About the Author

Abhishek is a storyteller with a keen eye for detail and a heart for high fantasy. Bringing a sharp legal perspective to the art of world-building, he creates immersive landscapes where logic meets the impossible.

In his debut series, The Glowsky Saga, he explores the enduring power of friendship and the deep-seated secrets of a world caught in the gears of time. For Abhishek, the most compelling cases aren't found in a courtroom, but in the journeys that stay with a reader long after the final page is turned.

Acknowledgments

Writing this book has been an incredible journey, and I am grateful to everyone who has supported me along the way. A special thanks to my family and friends for their unwavering belief in me. To all those who love stories of magic, mystery, and adventures this one is for you.

Prologue: Whispers of the Unknown

The wind howled through the towering spires of Glowsky, carrying whispers of forgotten secrets. The night was thick with mist, curling around the ancient stone walls like ghostly fingers. Somewhere in the depths of the great library, a candle flickered—its lonely flame casting restless shadows across the endless shelves of timeworn books.

A figure moved between them, careful, deliberate. The silence of the place was sacred, broken only by the soft rustling of parchment. There, buried beneath layers of dust, was a book that should not have been there. A book that had not been touched for centuries.

Its leather cover was cracked, its pages yellowed with age. Yet, there was something unsettling about it—something alive, as if the words inside were waiting to be read.

The figure hesitated, fingers grazing the spine. A strange sensation crawled up their arms, as though the book itself recognized them.

A quiet breath. A moment of uncertainty.

Then, they opened it.

And the secrets of Glowsky began to unravel.

TABLE OF CONTENTS

Chapter 1: The Whisper of Glowsky

The train shrieked as it slowed, its iron wheels grinding against the frostbitten tracks. A thick cloud of steam hissed into the frozen air, swallowed instantly by the dense mist that clung to the world like an old, forgotten memory. The cold was sharp, biting through wool and leather, sending shivers through the bones of anyone daring to stand outside. But there was no one.

The station emerged from the fog, a lonely relic of time, its wooden beams weathered and groaning under the weight of neglect. A faded gold sign swayed above the empty platform, the cold wind nudging it gently, its hinges creaking with a sound that felt almost like a whisper. GLOWSKY. The letters were peeling, worn down by the years, yet still standing, still marking a place that felt lost to the rest of the world.

Roffel Grayson stepped off the train, his black eyes flickering beneath the shadow of his hat. The muffler around his neck, old and tattered, coiled loosely like a serpent, fluttering faintly in the wind. His coat, heavy and dark, did little to keep the frost from creeping under his skin. His boots crunched against the fresh snow as he took his first steps onto the platform, feeling the weight of silence settle around him. The leather briefcase in his hand, its surface cracked, and edges frayed, seemed heavier than before. It had travelled with him for years, carrying things more valuable than mere papers.

Behind him, the train shuddered, its engine groaning one last time. A final exhale of steam escaped from its metal lungs before it lurched forward, disappearing into the mist. In mere moments, the only proof of its existence was the faint outline of its tracks, slowly vanishing beneath the fresh snowfall.

Roffel was alone.

Beyond the platform, a chariot awaited. It was a rickety thing of black wood and iron, standing eerily still as though it had been there for centuries. The horse, thin and gaunt, exhaled slow puffs of white, its ribs pressing starkly against its skin. It did not shift, did not paw at the ground. It simply waited.

The driver sat hunched, swathed in layers of fur, his face hidden beneath a heavy hood. He did not greet Roffel. He did not speak. He did not even turn his head. He simply tipped his chin slightly, a silent acknowledgment, a gesture that felt like an old agreement neither of them had made but both understood.

Roffel climbed into the chariot, settling into the stiff, frozen seat. The briefcase thudded against the wood beside him, its weight grounding him. Without a word, the driver flicked the reins, and the chariot jolted forward, its wheels slicing through the snow, carving deep grooves into the frostbitten ground.

The forest swallowed them.

The path twisted, winding deeper into the heart of the woods, where the air felt thicker, heavier, like a place the sun had abandoned long ago. The trees stood tall and bare, their blackened limbs reaching skyward like skeletal fingers, clawing at the gray expanse above. The wind whispered through the branches, carrying no warmth, only secrets long buried beneath the roots.

There were no birds, no rustling leaves, no distant sounds of life—only the relentless crunch of hooves against snow, a rhythm that seemed almost unnatural in its solitude.

Then, without warning, the chariot halted.

Roffel looked up.

Before him lay a clearing, small and secluded, wrapped in a tangle of twisted roots and frostbitten branches, as though nature itself was trying to keep something hidden. At its centre stood a hut—leaning slightly to one side, as if struggling to remain standing against time's pull.

Smoke curled from the stone chimney, thin and weak, like a dying breath fading into the cold air. The wooden walls, once sturdy, had succumbed to age, their surfaces warped and splintered.

Beneath the sagging eaves, waiting in the cold, stood Mathelda.

She was old—not merely in years, but in the way that ancient trees are old, in the way that mountains remember storms. Her face, a landscape of deep lines and hollows, peeked from beneath the folds of a Gray Woolen hood. Her silver eyes, sharp and unreadable, seemed to cut through the mist like twin blades.

In her hands, she gripped a gnarled wooden staff, its tip flickering with a faint, pulsing light, as if it held a dying ember of something far greater than fire.

"You're late," she rasped, her voice dry and brittle, like autumn leaves crushed beneath a heavy boot.

Roffel did not flinch. His voice was steady. "Trains don't bend to my will."

Mathelda's lips twitched—not quite a smile, not quite a frown. "Patience, boy." She turned toward the hut, her staff tapping softly against the frozen ground. "Come."

Inside, the air was thick. The scent of damp wood, old parchment, and something… older clung to the walls. Shelves overflowed with books, their spines cracked, their pages curled from time's relentless march. Glass jars lined the surfaces, filled with strange herbs, powders, and substances Roffel could not name.

A fire struggled to burn in the hearth, its embers pulsing weakly, casting flickering shadows across the room.

Mathelda moved toward a worn rug in the corner, her steps slow but sure. She knelt, her bony fingers tracing something in the dust. A low rumble trembled through the floor.

The wooden planks shifted.

Beneath the rug, a trapdoor yawned open, revealing a tunnel leading into the earth itself.

Without hesitation, Mathelda descended, her staff's glow casting eerie light against the slick stone walls. The tunnel twisted downward, curling like the veins of some buried beast.

Roffel followed.

The deeper they went, the heavier the air became. It pressed against his skin, whispering of something ancient, something powerful, something that had been waiting.

Finally, they reached a chamber.

Mathelda's staff flared, flooding the space with light. The walls shimmered, carved with runes that pulsed like a heartbeat. The shelves overflowed with books, their covers cracked, their pages whispering secrets.

But in the centre of the room, on a stone table, lay a single iron-bound box.

Its edges gleamed, its surface scarred, as if it had endured centuries of struggle.

Roffel's breath caught. His fingers hovered over the lock.

Mathelda's silver eyes gleamed. "But be warned, boy."

Her voice dropped, almost reverent.

"Open it… and there's no turning back."

The room fell silent.

Roffel set down his briefcase, its lock clicking softly.

Then, his hand moved forward—

And the secrets of Glowsky tightened their grip.

Chapter 2: Echoes of Tindle

A shrill alarm pierced the silence, shattering the dim chamber, the glowing runes, and the iron-bound box into fragments of shadow and mist.

Roffel jolted upright, his breath coming in ragged gasps, his heart hammering against his ribs. His black eyes darted around the room, searching—for what, he didn't know.

The hut was gone. Mathelda's piercing silver gaze had vanished. The briefcase, stamped with "Tindle" in faded script, dissolved into nothingness. Instead, he found himself staring at the ceiling of his small, cluttered bedroom.

The clock blinked 10:00 a.m., its red digits glaring accusingly in the dim light.

For a moment, the cold bite of Glowsky's air still clung to his skin, like a phantom refusing to let go. But as he sat there, the sensation faded, replaced by the damp warmth of reality. His T-shirt stuck to him, soaked in sweat, and the faint scent of ink and old paper lingered in the air—remnants of the open books strewn across his desk.

The same dream. Again.

The train, the forest, the old woman—it all felt too real to be a mere trick of sleep. He could still hear the howling wind through skeletal trees, still feel the weight of the iron-bound box in his hands. But like mist slipping through fingers, the details faded, dissolving into the ordinary world around him.

Was it a memory? A warning?

Roffel swung his legs over the bed, the wooden floor creaking underfoot. The small flat he shared with his mother was silent, save for the distant hum of the city beyond the frosted window. She had already left for work at the textile mill, just as she always did.

A note lay on the table, scrawled in her hurried script:

"Don't be late for college, Roff. Love, Mum."

He crumpled the paper absently, running a hand through his sleep-mussed hair before shuffling toward the bathroom. The splash of cold water on his face did little to chase away the unease coiling in his gut. His reflection stared back—dark circles beneath black eyes, lips pressed in a thin line, hair still ruffled from restless sleep.

With a sigh, he dressed quickly—jeans, a worn jacket, and his usual leather boots. His hand hovered over his scarf for a moment, the image of the muffler from his dream flashing in his mind.

But he left it behind.

The morning air was crisp, biting at his skin as he stepped outside. Though the sun had risen weakly over the horizon, its warmth did little to push back the lingering chill.

Down the street, a familiar figure leaned against a lamppost, arms crossed, impatience radiating from her stance.

Saerene Wenfield.

Her auburn hair was pulled back into a loose ponytail, strands of it catching the light like fire. Around her neck hung a small wing-shaped pendant, glinting in the pale sunlight.

She tapped her foot, her green eyes narrowing as he approached.

"You're late," she said flatly.

Roffel shrugged, stuffing his hands into his jacket pockets. "It's just orientation today. Professor Sproun won't care."

She rolled her eyes, falling into step beside him as they headed toward campus.

Saerene had been his closest friend since childhood—the one person who had remained a constant in his life, through the quiet strength of his mother and the absence of his father. She was sharp, quick-witted, and fearless, but something about her presence always made him feel grounded.

They climbed the hill toward Halewood College, their boots crunching over patches of frozen leaves.

Halewood had stood for over a century, its weathered brick walls carrying the weight of time. Unlike the modern institutions spreading through the city, Halewood clung to tradition—its halls lined with dusty tomes, its corridors filled with aging portraits of long-dead scholars.

Room 312 was tucked away on the third floor, its wooden door creaking in protest as they entered.

Inside, the lecture hall buzzed with voices, a mixture of new and returning students settling into their seats.

At the front, Professor Sproun—a wiry woman with sharp features and even sharper eyes. Her graying hair is always tied up in a messy bun, and her glasses perch at the end of her long, pointed nose. Her gaze is calculating, her words chosen carefully. She wears long, flowing robes in dark colours, usually adorned with strange symbols only she understands. Her bony fingers are covered in rings, and when she speaks, her voice is dry but always layered with meaning. She seems to know more than she lets on, and every sentence she utters feels like it carries a hidden warning..

She had a no-nonsense air about her, the kind that made students sit up straighter the moment she entered the room.

"Welcome to your new class!" she declared, a grin tugging at her thin lips. "You're not teenagers anymore—ha! Time to think bigger, dig deeper."

Roffel slid into a seat near the back, Saerene settling beside him.

The wing pendant at her throat caught the light again, flashing for a brief second before she tucked it beneath her sweater.

But Roffel wasn't paying attention.

His mind was still trapped in the dream.

The briefcase. The iron box.

The name Tindle, burned into leather like a brand.

What did it mean?

Saerene nudged him, her voice low. "You're zoning out again."

Roffel hesitated, then muttered, "Just a dream. Same one."

Her brow furrowed, concern flickering across her face. But before she could press further, Professor Sproun clapped her hands, silencing the room.

"Right!" she said. "Let's start with a question."

She turned to the chalkboard, scrawling the words in bold, sweeping strokes:

What drives you to unravel a mystery?

Roffel's hand twitched over his notebook.

He didn't raise it.

But the answer was already there.

Etched into his mind like an echo from the past.

Tindle.

Chapter 3: Shadows in Botenicalden

The city of **Botenicalden** lay hushed under a thin blanket of silver snow. Ancient stone buildings, draped in frozen ivy and winter mist, lined the streets like sleeping giants. The flickering gas lamps cast a warm, amber glow over the cobblestones, their light dancing on the frost. The morning air was sharp and biting, smelling of roasted chestnuts and the thick, heavy scent of coal smoke. Trams rumbled along their iron tracks, their bells ringing out through the quiet winter morning.

For **Roffel Grayson**, the city felt like a well-worn coat—familiar, yet somehow starting to feel too tight. He had walked these alleys his entire life, but today, the shadows felt longer. Perhaps it was the dream that refused to let him go.

Every night, it was the same haunting loop. *The train at Glowsky. The heavy briefcase marked "Tindle." The old woman, Mathelda, beckoning him into a tunnel of total darkness.* He would wake up with his heart drumming against his ribs, desperately trying to catch the details before they dissolved like smoke in the wind.

He pulled his jacket tighter against the chill. His mother had already left for her shift at the textile mill, leaving a small, handwritten note on the kitchen table: *"Don't be late, Roff. Love, Mum."* He folded the scrap of paper and tucked it into his pocket, a small piece of warmth against the cold.

The Inner Circle

At the school gates, **Saerene Wenfield** was waiting in her usual spot. She stood with her arms crossed, her auburn hair tied back in a messy knot, stray strands catching the pale winter sun. Around her neck, a small wing-shaped pendant glinted with a strange, soft light.

"You're late again," she noted, her voice sharp but playful.

Roffel sighed, his breath a cloud of white mist. "I was thinking."

"That's a dangerous hobby," she smirked, falling into step beside him.

They had been a team since they were tall enough to reach the door handles. Saerene was the fire to Roffel's water—quick-witted, fierce, and always the first to demand the truth. As they walked, the rest of their world joined them.

Kael, with his golden curls and easy smile, made the heavy morning feel lighter. **Lila** walked quietly, her fingers stained with charcoal from her sketchbook. **Marush**, the tallest of them all, walked like a silent guardian. They were children of Botenicalden, raised in its twisting alleys and gas-lit secrets. But lately, the air between them felt electric, as if they were all standing on the edge of a great cliff.

The Professor with the Piercing Eyes

Botenicalden High was a massive building of grey stone and frosted glass. Inside, the halls smelled of floor wax and old paper. The library, where their orientation was held, was a cathedral of books. Dust motes drifted through the sunlight, hovering over rows of leather-bound volumes that held centuries of forgotten knowledge.

Roffel took a seat at the back, but his attention was immediately snapped forward when the new professor entered.

Professor Elias Warrick was a man made of sharp angles and cold shadows. His silver-streaked black hair was slicked back perfectly, and his piercing blue eyes moved across the room like a hawk searching for prey. He wore a dark, immaculate suit and a heavy silver ring on his left hand. When he spoke, his voice was smooth as silk but firm as iron.

"Good morning, Year 11s," he said, his blue eyes pausing on Roffel for a heartbeat too long. "Welcome to Botenicalden High. It is time to stop playing at childhood. It is time to start thinking bigger."

Roffel barely heard the uneasy laughter of the other students. His eyes had drifted to a high, shadowed shelf. There, tucked away between two thick books, was a spine with faded gold letters:

The Tindle Chronicles.

Roffel's chest tightened. His hands turned ice-cold. *Tindle.* The name from the briefcase. The name from the dream.

The Discovery

When the orientation ended, Roffel didn't join the rush for the door. He walked straight to the shelf and pulled the book down. It was heavy, its blank pages yellowed and brittle with age. As he flipped it open, his heart nearly stopped.

Inside the back cover, there was a map marked in dark, permanent ink, with some landmarks on its surface which were of his nightmares: *The Forest. That Glowsky station.*

It wasn't just a dream. It was a trail.

"Found something interesting?"

Kael's voice made Roffel jump. His friends had gathered around him, their faces a mix of curiosity and concern. Roffel quickly closed the book, but he could still feel the warmth of the pages under his palm.

"Maybe," Roffel murmured, looking up to see Professor Warrick watching them from the front of the room, his expression unreadable.

Saerene leaned in, her wing-shaped pendant swinging forward. "What is it, Roff?"

Roffel looked at the snow falling silently outside the window. The name *Tindle* was no longer a whisper in his sleep. It was a reality waiting in the woods.

"I don't know yet," he said, his voice steady for the first time that morning. "But I'm going to find out."

Chapter 4: The Map's Call

The book wasn't just a coincidence. Finding it under that specific shelf felt like a deliberate sign—a jagged piece of the puzzle that had haunted Roffel's sleep for weeks. But there was a problem: the book lived in the **Restricted Section**, a dim-lit corner of the library marked *Professors Only*.

In that section, the lanterns flickered lower, and the air smelled of ancient dust. **Miss Harrow**, the library professor, guarded the aisles like a hawk. With her sharp eyes and bouncy gray curls, she never missed a thing. If a single page was turned too loudly, she would know. Stealing the book legally was impossible.

The Midnight Plan

That night, in the cramped warmth of Roffel's bedroom, the group gathered in a tight circle. The weak glow of a desk lamp turned their faces into a collection of golden masks and long shadows.

Roffel told them everything—the train, the briefcase, and the ghostly image of **Mathelda** leading him into the dark. His voice was low, and his hands tightened into fists as he showed them a rough sketch of what he had seen.

"We need that book," he said, his voice firm.

The silence lasted only a second. **Saerene** sat up straighter, her green eyes flashing with mischief. "Then we take it," she said, as if they were planning to steal an apple rather than a forbidden relic.

The plan was set for Friday. Marush would provide the distraction. Lila would prepare a fake book. Kael would be the lookout. And on Sunday, they would follow the map into the heart of the forest.

The Library Heist

Friday arrived, cold and sharp. The group moved through the library like clockwork.

Marush acted first. He moved his towering frame toward the heavy encyclopedias. Then—CRASH. A cascade of thick volumes slammed onto the wooden floor, sending a cloud of dust into the air.

"Mr. Marush!" Miss Harrow barked, her voice echoing off the high ceiling as she stormed over to scold him.

In that heartbeat of chaos, Saerene used a thin hairpin to click the lock open. Roffel slipped inside, his heart hammering against his ribs. He grabbed the book, his fingers trembling as he flipped through the brittle pages.

The first pages were blank, but on the third, words began to crawl across the paper as if written by an invisible ghost:

"To seek power is to understand the cost. To wield it is to control fate."

Roffel's breath hitched. Tucked deep inside the binding was a piece of thick, folded parchment. As he unfolded it, he saw thin, intricate lines that glowed with a faint, ghostly light. It showed the river, the trees, and a single, lonely point: **The Hut.** He ripped the map free, stuffed it into his jacket, and slipped out just as Miss Harrow turned back.

Into the Woods

Sunday morning was bleak and gray. Roffel's mother watched him with suspicious, careful eyes as he headed for the door. "Stay with me today, Roff," she pleaded softly.

Roffel swallowed hard, his heart heavy with the lie. "Seeing Saerene," he muttered, slipping out before she could say more.

The group met where the city streets died and the wild forest began. The trees loomed ahead, their bare branches twisting toward the gray sky like skeletal fingers. The air felt thick, as if the forest itself was holding its breath.

Marush noticed something different about Saerene. "No necklace today?" he asked, glancing at her bare throat.

Saerene touched her collarbone absentmindedly. "It's my mother's. I didn't want to risk losing it in the brush."

Roffel tightened his grip on the map. With a deep breath, they stepped off the path and into the tangled roots and icy brooks. With every step, the silence deepened. The city felt miles away, and a strange, ancient energy began to hum in the air.

They weren't just hiking. They were being pulled. And the name whispering through the dead leaves was **Tindle**.

<h1 style="text-align:center">Chapter 5: The Mark of Glowsky</h1>

The forest swallowed the morning light, leaving only a cold, gray gloom. Mist curled around the roots of the trees like white smoke, and the twisted branches reached out like skeletal arms. The air was heavy with the scent of damp earth and the biting sting of frost.

Roffel led the way, his fingers white-knuckled around the stolen map. Behind him, the group moved in a tight pack. Every crunch of a frozen leaf sounded like a gunshot in the unnatural silence. They were miles past the safe trails of Botenicalden now, entering a part of the woods that felt... *awake*.

The Buried Name

Suddenly, a sharp yelp broke the quiet. Lila had tripped, her knee slamming into the frozen ground.

"What the hell was that?" she hissed, brushing snow off her coat.

Roffel knelt beside her. He didn't see a rock or a root. Instead, something wooden was peeking through the frost beneath a cluster of thorns. It was a marker, gray and weathered by a hundred winters.

"Clear it," Saerene whispered, already reaching for the vines.

They pulled away the frozen weeds, their fingers numbing in the cold. As the dirt fell away, deep, jagged carvings appeared. The letters were old, but the name was unmistakable:

GLOWSKY

Roffel stared at it, his breath coming in ragged puffs. "I told you," he whispered, his voice hoarse. "In my dream, this was a station. A place where things begin. But out here... it looks like a grave."

Saerene's gloved fingers traced the wood. "It's ancient. Like something time tried to erase, but failed. We're close. We have to be."

The Empty Horizon

They pushed forward with new energy, following the map to its very end. But when they reached the final "X," they didn't find a magical hut or a dark tunnel.

They found nothing.

The land was barren, empty, and silent. No Mathelda. No station. Just a field of dead grass and biting wind.

"Alas," Lila sighed, dropping her satchel with a heavy thud. "I thought we'd be eating snacks in a cozy hut. Instead, we have... a lot of dirt." She pulled out an apple, but the joke fell flat.

Marush placed a heavy hand on Roffel's shoulder. "Maps can trick you, Roff. Maybe the ink moved. Maybe it's a dead end."

Defeated and shivering, they turned back. The forest felt even colder now, as if it were mocking them. Then, a sound emerged from the shadows.

A low, guttural growl.

Before anyone could scream, a blur of matted fur and yellow teeth lunged from the mist. A shabby, wild dog—its ribs showing through its skin—snapped at Roffel's leg. Pain exploded like white heat. Roffel fell back, his hands clawing at the mud as the dog's teeth sank deep.

Chaos erupted. Marush swung a heavy branch, and with one final snarl, the beast vanished back into the dark trees. Roffel lay on the ground, gasping, blood seeping into his jeans.

"Hospital," Saerene commanded, her face as pale as the snow. "Now!"

The Watchful Eye

The white walls of Botenicalden General were too bright, and the smell of bleach was sickening. Roffel lay on the crinkling paper of the hospital bed while his mother held his hand, her face a mask of terror.

But it was the man standing at the foot of the bed who made Roffel's blood run cold.

Professor Elias Warrick. The teacher stood perfectly still, his spectacles catching the clinical light.

"What happened?" his mother asked, her voice trembling.

"Dog attack," Roffel lied quickly, his mind racing. "On the street near the park."

Professor Warrick leaned forward slightly, his blue eyes piercing right through Roffel's soul. "You should be more careful roaming in the **forest**, Grayson. It's a treacherous place for those who don't know the way."

Roffel's heart skipped a beat. *The forest?* He had said the *street*. How did Warrick know?

The professor didn't say another word. He simply gave a thin, knowing smile and walked out, his polished shoes clicking rhythmically on the linoleum.

The Hidden Script

Days later, Roffel lay in his room at home. His leg was bandaged and throbbing, and his mother was downstairs, her silence heavy with suspicion.

He picked up the stolen map, staring at it with a frustrated scowl. "We followed it perfectly," he muttered. "Why was there nothing there?"

Angrily, he flipped the map over.

The light from his bedside lamp hit the back of the parchment at a sharp angle. For a second, he thought his eyes were playing tricks on him. Then, the ink began to shimmer.

It wasn't a stain. It was **writing**.

Faint, curling letters began to crawl across the back of the map. It wasn't English. It wasn't any language Roffel had ever seen in a schoolbook. The letters looked like twisted vines, glowing with a dull, dark purple light.

His heart hammered against his ribs. The map wasn't a failure. It was a **code**.

Tindle's name whispered in his mind again, but this time, it was accompanied by the strange, curling script on the paper. The journey hadn't ended in the empty field. It was only just being unlocked.

Chapter 6: The Riddle of Lumivara

The word *Lumivara* curled across the back of the map like a sleeping snake. It was hidden beneath the strange, vine-like script, its ink so faded that it seemed to belong to another century. But under the glow of Roffel's desk lamp, the letters stood out with a sudden, haunting clarity.

Roffel's leg throbbed with a dull, rhythmic pain, but he ignored it. His mind was racing. He grabbed his phone, his fingers trembling as he dialed Saerene.

"You won't believe this," he whispered into the receiver. "There's a word hidden in the fibers of the paper—*Lumivara*. The dream, the dog, the map... it's all one machine, and this word is the key."

Saerene's voice was calm, but he could hear the gears turning in her head. "Don't do anything reckless, Roff. Just rest. We'll figure it out together."

But rest was the last thing on Roffel's mind.

The Uninvited Guest

The next morning, a sharp, rhythmic knock startled Roffel. He hobbled to the door, his movements stiff. When he swung it open, his stomach dropped.

Professor Sproun.

She stood on his porch, her sharp eyes hidden behind thick spectacles. She looked wiry and intense, like a bird of prey. "How is the leg, Grayson?" she asked, her voice smooth—too smooth. "The school was worried about the... dog attack."

"Better, thanks," Roffel muttered, trying to block her view of the room.

But Sproun didn't move. Her gaze flickered past him, scanning his desk. For a split second, her eyes landed on the map. Her lips parted in a tiny gasp of recognition—a look of pure shock that she masked a second later with a fake smile.

"Take it easy, eh?" she said quickly, turning on her heel. She practically ran down the hallway.

Roffel stood frozen. *She knew that map.* She didn't just recognize it; she was afraid of it.

The Secret in the Library

While Roffel watched the door, Saerene and Lila were deep in the school library, dodging the hawk-like gaze of Miss Harrow. They moved through the shadows of the towering shelves until Saerene stopped at a heavy Latin glossary.

"Lumivara," Saerene whispered, her finger tracing the word. "It translates to *True Light*."

Lila frowned, sketching a quick symbol in her book. "True light? What does that mean? A flashlight? A fire?"

"I don't know yet," Saerene said, snapping the book shut. "But we're missing a piece of the puzzle."

Warrick's Shadow Play

Later that day, **Professor Warrick** paced the front of the classroom. The winter sun cast his shadow long and distorted against the chalkboard. He stopped suddenly and looked directly at Roffel.

"If a shadow moves without its source," Warrick said, his blue eyes cold and piercing, "what shifts first—the light or the intent?"

The room went silent. Roffel felt the weight of the question. It wasn't about physics; it was a test.

"Intent," Roffel answered, his voice steady. "Light is just the echo of what the mind decides to do."

A slow, dangerous smirk played on Warrick's lips. "Sharp, Grayson. Very sharp."

The Sun's Key

That night, the group gathered in Roffel's room. They tried everything. They held the map over a candle, hoping the heat would reveal the ink. Nothing. They tried lemon juice. Nothing.

"Damn it," Kael groaned, kicking the bedpost. "Maybe it's just old paper after all."

But the next morning, Saerene burst into the room, her eyes blazing with excitement. "I was wrong! It's not heat. *True Light* means the original source. The sun!"

She pulled the small golden wing-pendant from her neck. "My mother said this glass was special—it amplifies the sun's rays."

They rushed to the window just as the dawn broke over the rooftops of Botenicalden. Saerene held the map up, catching the first ray of pale morning light through the golden wings of her necklace.

A flare of brilliant gold light washed over the parchment.

The map shuddered in her hands. Ink began to bloom across the paper like blood spreading in water. The word *Lumivara* burned bright purple, and beneath it, the name **Glowsky** appeared in jagged, ancient letters.

Then, a route unfurled. A dark line snaked west from the marker they had found in the forest, leading to a circled hut, and then further north into a jagged, terrifying region labeled **The Veil.**

"Glowsky was just the entrance," Roffel whispered, his heart thundering. "The hut... and then the Veil. This is the whole path."

Kael's grin was wild and reckless. "Tomorrow evening. After school, when the teachers are busy. We follow the golden line."

They left the map on the desk, the ink still humming with a faint, magical energy. The forest was no longer just a place of trees and shadows. It was a doorway. And tomorrow, they were going to walk through it.

Chapter 7: Shadows After School

The afternoon sun bled through the dusty windows of the classroom, painting long, golden bruises across the wooden desks. **Professor Warrick** moved like a shadow against the chalkboard, his voice cutting through the restless murmurs of the students. He stopped suddenly, his sharp gaze pinning Roffel to his seat.

"If a door has no handle and no keyhole," Warrick asked, his blue eyes intense, "does it stay closed because of the lock, or because you believe it cannot be opened?"

The air in the room grew heavy. It wasn't a lesson in architecture; it was a challenge of the will. Roffel felt the dull throb in his bandaged leg, but his mind felt like a whetted blade.

"Belief," Roffel said, his voice ringing out clearly. "A lock only exists if you accept the boundary. If the intent is strong enough, the door is already open."

Warrick stared at him for a long beat. A flicker of something—recognition, perhaps—crossed his face before his mouth curved into a ghost of a smile. "Sharp, Grayson. A mind that sees past the frame is a dangerous thing. Keep it honed."

The Venom of the Trio

As the class began to pack up, **Kael** leaned over with his signature smirk. "What's next, Professor Door-Opener? Planning to walk through walls for extra credit?"

Lila stifled a laugh, already sketching a cartoon of Roffel walking through a solid brick wall, while Marush let out a low rumble of amusement. But the laughter was cut short by a voice that sounded like grinding stones.

"Hey, Gimp—heard a stray mutt trying to turn you into lunch."

Roffel didn't have to look. He knew that lazy, arrogant drawl anywhere. Jace Korran stood there, his athletic frame blocking the sunlight. Beside him, Tessa Varkis braided her dark hair with fingers covered in black leather gloves, her eyes gleaming with cruelty. Gav Renn stood behind them, a wall of mindless muscle, letting out a guttural, mocking bark.

"What's it like being dog chow, pup?" Tessa sneered, her voice dripping with venom.

Roffel's fists whitened at his sides. He felt a cool touch on his arm—Saerene. Her silver wing-pendant caught the light as she leaned in. "They're just noise, Roff," she whispered. "Don't give them the satisfaction."

Warrick's voice snapped across the room like a whip. "Korran, Varkis—quiet, or you'll spend your weekend in detention." The room went silent, but as Warrick looked at Roffel, his gaze felt strangely protective, almost like a guardian watching over a cub.

The Broken Threshold

The next evening, as the shadows of Botenicalden stretched into long, thin fingers, the group arrived at Roffel's house. But the usual warmth of home was gone. The front door stood slightly ajar, swaying in the cold wind with a rhythmic *creak-creak*.

A heavy sense of dread settled in Roffel's chest. He pushed the door open.

His room was a nightmare.

Books had been ripped from their shelves, their spines snapped. Drawers were overturned, spilling clothes and personal trinkets like internal organs across the floor. His mattress had been slashed open, the stuffing scattered like snow.

Marush stepped over the wreckage, his heavy boots crunching on broken glass. He scanned the room with a soldier's eyes. "Whoever did this wasn't looking for money," he said, his voice low and dangerous. "They were looking for *it*."

Roffel scrambled toward his desk, his breath coming in short, panicked gasps. He reached for the hidden compartment where he had tucked the parchment.

His hand met empty wood.

"The map," Roffel whispered, his voice cracking with a mix of fury and fear. "It's gone. They took it."

Chapter 8: Echoes and Suspicions

Roffel was drowning in a dream of thick, suffocating fog. The darkness wasn't just an absence of light; it was a predator, shifting around his boots with a hungry intent. From the haze, a voice rasped his name—low, ancient, and bone-chilling.

"Roffel... Roffel..."

Mathelda emerged from the mist, her gray cloak tattered like the wings of a moth. Her eyes burned like dying embers. She didn't speak with her mouth; her voice slithered directly into his skull. She pointed a bony, trembling finger at an iron box, rusted and bound in heavy, groaning chains.

Something inside the box thudded. *Boom. Boom.* Like a trapped heartbeat.

Suddenly, the shadows fractured. Cloaked figures lunged from the fog, blades silver and cold. Roffel ducked a slashing dagger, his fist connecting with a faceless attacker. As the chaos peaked, Mathelda's cackle tore through the air. The earth groaned and split open, and from the dirt, a crooked wooden hut rose like a jagged tooth.

"Find it fast...," she hissed.

Waking to the Ruin

Roffel jolted upright, his sheets soaked with sweat. The phantom pain in his leg anchored him to the room, but the room itself was wrong. The moonlight revealed a disaster: drawers hanging open like broken jaws, papers scattered like fallen leaves.

The desk was bare. The map—the golden path to the Veil—was gone.

Mathelda's warning echoed in his ears. He didn't just want answers anymore; he needed them to survive.

The Library Heist

At dusk, the group huddled in the school courtyard. The air was biting, and the last streaks of purple sun were dying behind the spires of Botenicalden High.

"We hit the library tonight," **Saerene** whispered, her silver necklace pulsing with a faint, rhythmic light. "Someone knew exactly what was in that room. We check the restricted log—we see who touched *The Tindle Chronicles* before us."

Kael let out a nervous, sharp laugh. "Breaking into a locked library in the middle of the night? My resume is getting impressive."

They moved like shadows through the silent halls. Kael knelt at the massive oak doors, a paperclip in his steady hands. *Click.* The lock surrendered.

Inside, the library was a cathedral of silence. The towering shelves seemed to lean inward, whispering as the group passed. **Marush** stood by the door, a silent sentinel, while **Lila** clutched her pencil as if it were a dagger.

Roffel and Saerene reached the librarian's desk. Roffel flipped through the heavy leather log, his heart hammering against his ribs. He stopped. His blood went cold.

"Warrick," Roffel breathed, the name tasting like ash. "He was there before us. He knew the book wasn't blank."

"He's been watching you, Roff," Kael whispered, looking over his shoulder into the dark aisles. "The guy has been two steps ahead of us the whole time."

The Ghostly Lure

They turned to flee, but the darkness between the shelves didn't stay dark. A sphere of bluish light suddenly flared in the air, hovering like a ghost. It pulsed with a cold, magnetic energy, drifting slowly deeper into the library.

"What the hell is that?" Kael whispered, stepping back.

The light didn't answer. It drifted, beckoning them. They followed, their feet moving as if pulled by invisible wires. At the very back of the library, the light stopped before a blank, windowless wall—and vanished.

Then, the wood began to groan.

The stone and timber shifted, grinding together until a door appeared where there had been nothing but solid wall. It was ancient, carved with swirling patterns that seemed to move if you looked at them too long. The air around it crackled with a static charge that made their hair stand on end.

"That... that wasn't there before," Lila stammered, her pencil slipping from her numb fingers.

Saerene's necklace began to hum, a low vibration that Roffel could feel in his own chest. "It's calling us," she said, her voice a ghost of itself.

Roffel stared at the handle. Mathelda's hut. The iron box. The stolen map. Every path led to this door. He reached out, his hand steady despite the fear.

"Let's go," he said.

One by one, they stepped through the threshold, leaving the world of Botenicalden behind and entering a darkness that had been waiting for them for centuries.

Chapter 9: Secrets in the Dust

The wooden door groaned as it swung shut, the sound echoing like a tomb closing. The air in the storeroom was heavy, stale, and sour with the scent of centuries-old decay. Roffel felt his skin prickle; the shadows here didn't just sit—they seemed to breathe. Somewhere in the back of his mind, **Mathelda's** rasping voice from his dream continued to whisper, a low warning he couldn't quite ignore.

Suddenly, a golden spark fractured the darkness. **Saerene's necklace** flared briefly, its light cutting through the gloom like a knife. The glow cast jagged, skeletal shapes across the sagging walls, making the ancient wooden beams look like the ribs of a giant beast.

Dust covered every surface like a thick, gray shroud. Shelves stood in crooked, warped lines, stuffed with leather-bound books that smelled of ozone and rot. These weren't just books; they were relics of a forgotten world.

The Hall of Hollow Eyes

"Feels like a grave," **Kael** whispered, his breath coming out in a silver mist.

Marush stepped forward, his heavy boots crunching against the grit. His broad frame was tense, his hand resting near his belt. "It's too still," he muttered. "Even the dust feels... wrong."

They moved cautiously until the narrow passage opened into a massive, cavernous hall. Roffel spotted a rusted *Mashal*—an old torch—resting in a wall bracket. He struck a match. The fire hissed and sputtered before settling into a steady, flickering orange flame that danced across the room.

High above, moonlight bled through a cracked skylight, silver beams cutting through the haze. In the half-light, they saw them: **Portraits.**

Rows of paintings hung askew on the walls, their gold frames peeling. The faces were faded, their eyes hollow and haunting. Magicians of an era long dead. Roffel stopped before a painting of a young girl with a small, delicate tiara. He wiped the nameplate with his sleeve.

Alaska.

"Who is she?" Lila whispered, her sketchbook trembling in her hand. Roffel shook his head, moving to the next. A stern woman with cold, unreadable eyes.

Grenstein.

Roffel pulled a brittle book from a nearby shelf. The ink was so faded it looked like it was made of shadow. He read aloud: *"Tindle—defeated his rival in a clash of cunning, claimed the Guardian's Award, and protected the weak."* The words sounded noble, but in the flickering torchlight, they felt heavy—like a lie disguised as history.

The Face of the Principal

Marush pointed toward a smaller, more recent-looking painting. It showed a group of people standing together. Alaska had a majestic phoenix on her shoulder; Grenstein held a small, silver-eyed deer. Tindle stood with a sharp-eyed black cat curled in his arms.

But it was the man at the very edge of the frame that made their blood turn to ice. He had a sharp, familiar jawline and a gaze that demanded order.

Marush squinted, his brow furrowing. "Wait... is that Professor Harold Wood?"

Kael leaned in, his eyes widening. "It is. Younger, but it's definitely him. Our Principal is in an ancient magician's portrait?"

A strange, freezing chill swept through the group. Why was the head of their school standing alongside legends who had been dead for a hundred years?

The Revelation

Saerene walked toward a much larger portrait at the center of the hall, hidden under a tattered, moldy cloth. Her necklace began to hum, the golden wings pulsing against her skin with a frantic energy.

"Help me," she whispered, her voice cracking.

Together, they gripped the heavy fabric and pulled. A massive cloud of dust billowed into the air, swirling like ghosts in the torchlight. Roffel reached out and wiped the grime from the center of the canvas.

As the face was revealed, a collective gasp filled the cavernous room.

A man stood there, lean and tall, holding a wand like a scepter. His black hair was slicked back, streaked with silver at the temples. His piercing blue eyes seemed to look through the canvas and straight into Roffel's soul.

The name carved into the gold plate below hit them like a physical blow:

E L I A S W A R R I C K

But beneath the name, in smaller, older letters, was the title the book had just described.

T I N D L E

The room went deathly silent. Lila's sketchbook slipped from her fingers, hitting the dusty floor with a dull thud. Kael let out a strangled breath. Roffel's throat felt like it was closing.

The man who had stolen the map. The man who had accessed the chronicles. Their professor.

Roffel's voice was a hoarse, terrified whisper. "He isn't just our teacher. He *is* Tindle."

The Weight of the Truth

Marush's jaw tightened, his fists balling at his sides. "How? Tindle is supposed to be a hero from the past. How is he standing in our classroom?"

Saerene's necklace was vibrating now, a low, warning growl of energy. "And if he's Tindle... then the book we read was a lie. He didn't save the world. He took it."

Roffel looked back at the crooked hut in his mind. The dream was no longer a mystery; it was a map to a crime that was still happening. In the dying light of the torch, one thing was terrifyingly clear:

The man teaching them magic was the very monster they were trying to stop.

Chapter 10: Cracks in the Code

The silver dust of the storeroom still clung to their coats like ghostly fingerprints as they stood beneath the portrait of **Elias Tindle Warrick**. The name seemed to vibrate with a dark energy, mocking their confusion.

Saerene was the first to find her voice, though it was sharp with frustration. "It doesn't add up. I grew up respecting Tindle—he was a legend. He protected the weak; he built the foundations of our magic. Why would he steal his own map from his own book? It's a riddle inside a circle, and my brain is starting to hurt."

Roffel gripped the old chronicles, the leather cold against his palms. "Maybe it isn't his," he whispered. "Or maybe the hero in these pages is a mask for something much darker."

"Whatever it is, we need to move," **Marush** commanded, his voice a low rumble. "No one speaks of what we saw. Not a word."

Caught in the Steel Gaze

They retreated through the dark library, their shadows stretching like ink across the floor. But as they reached the main oak doors, the world stopped.

Miss Harrow.

She stood framed by the moonlight, her arms crossed and her eyes glowing like cold steel. The silence that followed was suffocating.

"Explain yourselves," she said, her voice a dangerous, quiet rasp. "Why are five students lurking in a restricted wing at midnight? Don't bother lying. This will likely be your last night at this college."

Lila's breath hitched. Kael's jaw dropped. They had survived a dog attack and a supernatural door, only to be defeated by a school rule.

The Interrogation

The next morning, the sunlight in Miss Harrow's office felt like a spotlight in an interrogation room. She sat behind her desk, her gaze cutting through them like a blade.

"Empty your pockets. What did you steal?" she demanded.

"Nothing," Saerene said, her voice remarkably steady. "Check the shelves. Every book is exactly where it belongs."

Harrow narrowed her eyes. "Then why was the restricted seal broken? You had no permission to be there."

Kael leaned toward Lila, a panicked whisper escaping his lips. "The shelf... you forgot to slide the hidden panel back." Lila's face turned the color of ash.

"Enough!" Harrow snapped, rising from her chair. "I am taking you to Principal Wood. Pack your bags."

But as she reached for the door, a smooth, firm voice stopped her.

"That won't be necessary, Professor Harrow."

Professor Warrick stood in the doorway, his lean frame draped in a dark, immaculate suit. He looked calm, but his eyes held an unnatural intensity. "I will handle this. Thank you for your diligence, but this is a... private matter regarding my curriculum."

Harrow hesitated, her eyes flickering between Warrick and the students, before giving a stiff nod and stepping aside.

The Mask Slips

Warrick led them into an empty classroom and locked the door. He turned to face them, his expression unreadable. "Tell me," he said softly. "What did you take?"

Roffel's temper finally snapped. The stress of the theft, the dream, and the injury boiled over. "You're the thief! You trashed my room! You stole the map because you knew we cracked the code—we know about **Lumivara**! We know your name is Tindle! Who are you really?"

Warrick didn't yell. He didn't even flinch. Instead, he looked genuinely stunned. He took a slow step back, his eyes darkening with a flurry of emotions.

"You... you reached **Lumivara**?" his voice was a whisper, filled with a strange, haunting relief. "I thought no one would ever find that path again."

The anger in the room evaporated, replaced by a confused silence. Warrick didn't look like a villain; he looked like a man who had been searching for something lost for a very long time.

"The map was stolen, yes," Warrick said, looking more to himself than to them. "But not by me. If you've unlocked the Lumivara, then the stakes are higher than I feared." He looked at Roffel, his gaze searching. "Was there anything else on the map? Any other markers?"

Roffel hesitated, looking at Saerene. "Just the forest... the hut... and a word we couldn't solve: **The Veil**."

To their utter shock, Warrick smiled. It wasn't the smirk of a predator; it was the soft, weary smile of a teacher who had finally seen a student succeed.

"Good," he whispered. "That is very good. Now, go to your classes. Professor Sproun is away, so I will be taking her lecture. But Roffel—meet me at my home this evening. Alone."

As they walked to the lecture hall, Saerene's mind was spinning. "If he didn't steal it, then who did? And why does he act like a stranger to his own history?"

Lila sighed, leaning against the cold stone wall. "I'm too tired for more riddles. Let's just survive his lecture first."

But Roffel could still feel the weight of Warrick's gaze. The "Tindle" from the books was a hero. The "Tindle" in the portrait was a legend. But the man in the classroom? He was a man with a secret that was about to change Roffel's life forever.

Chapter 11: Blood and Secrets

The evening shadows crawled across the quiet street like ink as Roffel approached Professor Warrick's house. The wooden steps groaned under his boots, and the wind hissed through the bare trees, sounding like a thousand overlapping whispers.

Roffel took a steadying breath and knocked. The door swung inward, revealing Warrick's tall frame silhouetted against the amber glow of a desk lamp. For the first time, the Professor's sharp expression softened. He stepped aside, gesturing for Roffel to enter.

The room breathed with the scent of old parchment and melted beeswax. Towering stacks of books acted like pillars, and ancient maps were pinned to the walls like butterfly specimens. In the corner, Roffel's eyes snagged on a weathered wooden box. It was latched tight, looking heavy with the weight of years.

A Conversation in the Dark

"Thanks," Roffel said, his voice sounding small in the quiet room. "For saving us from Harrow today. She would have finished us."

Warrick's mouth twitched into a ghost of a smile. "You are worth more than her temper, Roffel. Sit. Tell me what is burning in your mind."

Roffel sat, but his eyes kept drifting back to that mysterious box in the corner. "What's in there?"

Warrick followed his gaze, his expression flickering for a fraction of a second—a shadow of a secret. "Old photos," he said casually. "Pieces of a life before this one. I'll show you... eventually."

He leaned forward, his blue eyes intense. "But we aren't here for my old photos. What are you seeing, Roffel?"

The Visions That Won't Stop

Roffel let out a breath he felt he'd been holding for days. "I keep seeing her. Mathelda. She's in a tattered gray cloak, calling my name in a voice that sounds like dry leaves. There's a crooked hut and an iron box that thuds... like a trapped heart."

Warrick's jaw tightened. He didn't interrupt.

"Last night," Roffel continued, his voice growing sharper, "a black train rolled through the fog, screaming steam into the night. Mathelda told me to find the hut—or it would find me." He paused, his gaze turning accusatory. "And how did you know we were in the forest? I never told a soul. Not even my mother."

Warrick rubbed a hand over his tired face. "That was Professor Sproun. She saw you heading toward the tree line and came to me. She knew you were wandering into a storm you weren't ready for."

Roffel's gut twisted. *Sproun.* Why was she watching him so closely? But before he could dwell on it, Warrick's voice dropped into a low, somber tone.

The Guardian's Truth

"Listen to me, Roffel. I am the Guardian of Glowsky. It is not just a name on a map; it is a city of pure magic, folded away from the eyes of ordinary people. Sixteen years ago, the sky broke. Evil sorcerers rose to burn the city to the ground. We fought... and we lost."

Warrick's eyes darkened, lost in the smoke of old memories. "This college? It was once the heart of that magic. Most of it is sealed now, hidden behind stones and silence. But the hut you saw—the one in your dreams—is the source of it all. If the Dark Ones find it, they become unstoppable."

Roffel's heart hammered. "You hid the location in the Chronicles," he realized. "The Lumivara. The Veil. You locked it away."

Warrick nodded grimly. "I wove a spell into that ink so powerful that only I could ever call it back. Or... someone of my own life-force." He paused, looking at Roffel with a raw, trembling intensity. "How did the words appear for you, Roffel? You didn't have the key."

"I just... held it," Roffel whispered. "The words started crawling across the page when my fingers touched the paper."

Warrick stood slowly, the lamplight making him look older, more fragile. "There is only one reason the magic would answer to you."

A Shocking Revelation

Roffel frowned, the air in the room suddenly feeling very thin. "What are you saying?"

Warrick crossed the room in two long strides. His voice was a heavy whisper, thick with sixteen years of repressed emotion. "It's the blood, Roffel. The same blood that runs through my veins is screaming inside yours."

Roffel felt the floor tilt beneath him.

"I wove the map to recognize my bloodline," Warrick said, his hands reaching out to grip Roffel's shoulders. "The spell didn't break because you were clever. It broke because you are my son."

The words hit Roffel like a thunderclap. *Son.* "Your... son?" Roffel rasped, his world spinning into a kaleidoscope of impossible truths.

Warrick didn't answer with words. He pulled Roffel into a fierce, desperate hug. "Roffel Tindle," he murmured into his hair. "That is your name. I thought I had lost you to the shadows forever."

For the first time, the mask of the stern Professor shattered. Tears glinted in Warrick's eyes. "I hid you with Ellen to keep you safe from the fallout of the war. I gave you a different name to keep the wolves away from your door."

He pulled back, his grip tightening, his face turning urgent. "You must tell no one. Not the others. Not even Ellen. The moment you broke that seal, the Dark Ones felt the ripple. They know the bloodline is alive."

Warrick's voice dropped to a terrifying whisper. "They can sense you now, Roffel. You aren't just a student anymore. You are a target."

Chapter 12: Shadows Closing In

The morning sunlight filtered through the school's cracked windows in pale, dusty streaks. As Roffel walked through the gates with Kael, Saerene, and Marush, he felt a strange, humming energy in his chest.

The truth from the night before—that he was **Roffel Tindle**, the son of the Guardian—felt like a heavy, golden secret. It made the familiar stone hallways look different, as if he were seeing the world in high definition for the first time.

Kael nudged him, a grin splitting his face. "What's up with you, Roff? You're practically vibrating. Did you find a shortcut to the Veil in your cereal bowl?"

Roffel forced a shrug, keeping his face neutral. "Just... a good night's sleep. I'll tell you later."

But the lighter mood vanished the moment they stepped into the classroom. **Professor Sproun's** desk was a barren island. No wiry frame, no sharp, smirking lectures.

Saerene's silver necklace caught a stray beam of light as she scanned the empty chairs. "Second day now," she whispered, her brow furrowing. "And look... **Lila** isn't here either."

Marush's massive arms were crossed tightly over his chest. "Lila never misses a morning. She said she had sketches to finish, but this isn't like her."

Kael's grin died. "The map is stolen, Sproun vanishes, and now Lila? The timing is too perfect to be an accident."

The Office of Shadows

Between periods, they huddled in a shadowed corner of the hallway.

"We need that map back," Roffel said, his voice dropping to a low, hard edge. He looked at his friends, deciding how much to reveal. "Warrick told me something last night. Sproun was the one who tipped him off about the dog attack in the forest. The night I got my leg torn up."

Kael's eyes widened. "Wait... how could she possibly know? We didn't tell a soul."

"Exactly," Roffel said. "She was there. Or she sent it."

Saerene's expression turned dark and dangerous. "She's the one. She took the map, and now she's gone to ground."

"Then we start with her office," Marush rumbled, his eyes darting to the hallway monitors. "If she's a thief, she's left a trail."

They slipped into the faculty wing during lunch, moving like ghosts to avoid Jace Korran's mocking crew. When they reached Sproun's office, they found the door—unusually—unlocked.

The room felt like a cold, still grave. A massive portrait of a deer stared at them from the wall, its glass eyes unblinking and ancient. The shelves were a chaotic mess of rune-covered carvings and dust-covered globes.

Saerene rifled through a stack of papers on the desk and suddenly froze. She pulled out a crumpled scrap of parchment. "*Glowsky—West Ridge, Dusk.*" She looked up, her voice trembling. "This is it. The starting point for the hut's route."

Kael let out a sharp hiss. He pointed to an open journal on the shelf. The entry for the night of the burglary simply read: ***'Blood stirs.'***

Roffel's stomach lurched. She hadn't just stolen the map; she had been watching his house. She had smelled his bloodline the moment it woke up.

"We go to the forest," Marush said, his voice heavy with certainty. "Tonight. After the final bell."

The Breaking Point

The rest of the day was a blur of ticking clocks and rising dread. When the bell finally rang, Roffel didn't wait. He sprinted home, his mind racing with what he would need for the night ahead.

He burst through his front door, but he didn't even have time to drop his bag before the door flew open again.

Saerene stood there, gasping for air, her face the color of bone. Her eyes were wide, darting with a terror Roffel had never seen in her.

"Roffel!" she choked out, her hands shaking so hard she had to grab the doorframe to stay upright.

Roffel froze, his heart hammering against his ribs. "What happened? Are you okay?"

"No," Saerene sobbed, her voice cracking. "I went to check her house. I went to find her... but she's gone, Roffel. **Lila has been missing since yesterday evening.**"

The silence that followed was absolute. The "adventure" had just become a rescue mission. The forest wasn't just a place of secrets anymore; it was a hunting ground.

Sproun. The Map. And now Lila.

The shadows of Glowsky weren't just calling them—they were starting to take them, one by one.

Chapter 13: Secrets Unravelling

At the edge of the city, where the asphalt of Botenicalden met the gnarled roots of the West Ridge, Roffel stopped. He turned to his friends, his expression harder than it had ever been.

"We can't all go," he said, his voice steady. "If Sproun is watching the forest, she'll see a crowd. We need to be smart." He looked at **Kael and Marush**. "Go to Lila's house. Her mother is alone and terrified. Stay with her. If Lila calls, or if anyone approaches that house, I need to know instantly."

Marush nodded, his jaw set. "And the school?"

"Keep your ears open," Roffel instructed. "If the faculty starts acting strange, find us. Saerene and I are heading into the deep brush."

The House of Broken Silence

Marush and Kael reached Lila's doorstep as the sky turned the color of a fresh bruise. When the door opened, Lila's mother looked like a ghost of herself. Her eyes were swollen, and she clutched a dish towel as if it were the only thing keeping her upright.

"We're here about Lila," Marush said softly.

The woman's lips trembled. "She called me... last night," she whispered, her voice cracking like dry glass. "She said she was finishing some work at the college. She sounded... hurried. And then the line went dead. Where is my daughter?"

Kael reached out, his usual jokes gone, replaced by a rare gravity. "We don't have her yet, ma'am. But we aren't stopping until we do. Stay strong. We're staying right here with you."

The Breath of the Dragon

Deep in the westward woods, the air grew unnaturally still. The trees were thicker here, their branches weaving together to block out the fading sun. Roffel's chest felt warm—the hidden rhythm of his blood pulsing in time with the ancient forest.

Searing heat suddenly tore through the silence.

A roar of orange flame erupted from the shadows behind them, turning the mist into steam. The fire hissed as it licked the damp leaves, heading straight for Roffel's back. Before he could even draw a breath to scream, Saerene moved.

She didn't run. She stepped *into* the path of the flames. With a sharp flick of her wrist, a wave of brilliant, bluish light exploded from her palms. The fire didn't just stop—it dissolved, swallowed by a shimmering azure shield that smelled of rain and ozone.

"No time to gawk!" Saerene yelled, grabbing Roffel's wrist. "RUN!"

The Shelter of Stone

They bolted through the undergrowth, the forest a blur of gray and brown. From the canopy above, another strike of fire whistled toward them like a falling star.

Saerene didn't stop running; she threw a blind arc of blue energy over her shoulder. A sharp *BOOM* echoed through the valley as the two magics collided, shattering a nearby oak tree.

She dived toward a hidden outcropping of rock, pulling Roffel down into a shallow, moss-covered cave. They hit the dirt hard, gasping for air as the sound of heavy footsteps faded into the distance.

In the dark, damp silence of the cave, Saerene's necklace was the only light. It pulsed with a rhythmic, sapphire glow.

"I... I'm sorry," she whispered, her chest heaving. "For keeping it from you. The magic. I didn't know if you were ready to see it."

Roffel leaned his back against the cold stone, watching the blue light dance in her eyes. He wasn't shaking. He wasn't even surprised.

"You don't have to apologize," Roffel said quietly.

Saerene frowned, her brow furrowing in the dim light. "You aren't shocked? I just blocked a fireball with my bare hands, Roff."

"I saw the portrait, Saerene," Roffel admitted, his voice steady. "In the hidden chamber behind the library. There was a woman standing beside a great white horse. She was wearing that exact wing-pendant. She had your eyes."

Saerene's breath hitched. The sapphire glow of the necklace intensified for a second before softening. "My mother," she whispered. "She told me to keep it hidden until there is any danger. She said the necklace would know when it was time."

She looked at him, a new kind of respect in her gaze. "Then it's true. You were never an outsider, Roffel. You were the heartbeat this world was waiting for."

Roffel clenched his fists, the heat of his father's legacy burning in his veins. "Then let's stop hiding in caves. If Lila is out there, and Sproun is using fire to keep us away, it's time we showed them what the 'heartbeat' can really do."

Chapter 14: The Battle in the Forest

The silence of the cave was shattered not by a sound, but by a sudden, unnatural drop in temperature. A freezing gale swept through the forest, carrying the scent of dead leaves and ancient iron. At the mouth of the cave, the moonlight was abruptly blotted out.

A silhouette stood there—tall, jagged, and terrifying.

Professor Sproun stepped into the faint blue glow of the necklace. She was no longer the wiry history teacher in a tweed jacket. She wore a heavy, flowing cloak of midnight silk, its hem stitched with silver runes that pulsed like a dying heartbeat. Her eyes didn't just look at them; they burned with a predatory hunger.

"You have wandered far off the path of the mundane, children," Sproun said, her voice sounding like two stones grinding together. "You were never meant to find this door."

Roffel stepped forward, placing himself between the darkness and Saerene. The adrenaline masked the ache in his leg. "Where is Lila? We know you took the map, and we know you took her."

Sproun let out a low, melodic laugh that sent a chill through the stone walls. "Lila? You think I am the only shadow in these woods? You are playing a game where you don't even know the players." She raised a hand, her silver rings catching the light. "And players who don't know the rules... get removed."

Without a flick of a wand, a bolt of jagged, violet energy tore through the air.

The Duel in the Deep

Saerene reacted with the speed of a lightning strike. She threw her hands upward, and a translucent dome of sapphire light erupted around them. The dark bolt hit the shield with the sound of a cannon blast, sending sparks of violet and blue dancing across the cave ceiling.

Sproun's eyes narrowed, a flash of genuine surprise crossing her face. "So, the blood of the Horse-Queen is not yet thin. Impressive."

With a violent gesture, Sproun slammed her palms into the earth. The ground groaned as **black chains of shadow** erupted from the dirt, hissing like vipers as they lunged for Saerene's ankles. Saerene dived to the left, rolling over the jagged stones and coming up with her palms charged. She fired a streak of blue lightning that illuminated the entire forest, but Sproun simply swiped it away with a sleeve of her cloak.

The Professor countered with a massive wave of concussive force. Saerene blocked it, but the power was overwhelming. She was thrown back against the stone wall, her breath escaping in a pained gasp.

Sproun didn't give her a chance to recover. She turned her cold gaze to Roffel. She sneered. "Let's see if your light is as bright as your friend."

A spear of condensed darkness shot toward Roffel's chest. He tried to twist away, but it was too fast. The energy grazed his shoulder, tearing through his jacket and skin like a red-hot blade. Roffel hit the ground, his vision swimming in white pain.

The Awakening

"ROFFEL!" Saerene's scream echoed through the cave.

Seeing the blood on Roffel's arm triggered something primal in her. The sapphire pendant at her throat didn't just glow; it detonated. A pillar of blue light hit the ceiling, and Saerene rose to her feet, her eyes glowing with the intensity of a summer sky.

Sproun stepped back, her arrogance finally replaced by fear. "No... that power... it's too soon!"

Saerene didn't use a bolt or a blast. She reached out with both hands and *closed* them. A cage of shimmering blue bars erupted from the floor around Sproun, locking her in a prison of pure, vibrating energy.

Sproun threw herself against the bars, but the magic burned her. "You fool!" she screamed, her face contorting. "You don't understand the weight of that map! If you take it to the Veil, you are opening a door that can never be shut!"

Roffel pushed himself up. To his amazement, the searing pain in his shoulder was vanishing. Underneath his torn sleeve, the skin was knitting back together, glowing with a faint, golden warmth. His blood was healing itself.

He ignored Sproun's screams and lunged for her fallen cloak. His fingers closed around a familiar bundle of parchment. **The Map.**

"I'm ending this," Roffel said, his voice hard as iron. He turned to Saerene, who was trembling from the effort of holding the cage. "Keep her down. I'm going to be the only person who can lock this map forever."

The Guardian's Burden

Roffel sprinted through the forest, the trees a blur of motion as his rejuvenated legs carried him faster than he had ever run. He didn't stop until he reached the heavy oak door of Warrick's home. He burst inside, gasping for air, his lungs burning.

Professor Warrick looked up, his eyes wide with shock. "Roffel? What happened to you?"

Roffel didn't say a word. He stepped forward and slammed the parchment onto the desk. "I found it. I took it back from Sproun."

For a long moment, Warrick simply stared at the map. His hands trembled as he touched the edges of the paper. A look of immense, fatherly pride broke through his stern mask. "That's my boy," he whispered, his eyes gleaming. "Put it down. Let me see the damage."

Warrick's face darkened as he checked Roffel's shoulder, seeing the shredded jacket but the perfectly healed skin. "So, Sproun was the viper in the nest. I should have seen the signs... the way she watched you in the halls."

Roffel straightened his back. "We have to go back. Saerene has her trapped, but she said something about the Veil. She said the map is a door."

Warrick's expression turned deathly serious. He picked up a quill and began to trace new lines over the ink of the map.

"Listen to me, Roffel. If Sproun is working for the Dark Ones, the location of the Hut and vein is no longer safe. I must rewrite the geography of the Vein immediately. I am going to shift the Hut's location—move it deep into the shifting folds of the forest where no one, not even Sproun, can track it."

He looked his son in the eye, his voice firm. "It is the only way to protect the source of our magic. But I cannot leave this desk until the ritual is finished. You must go back to Saerene. She is holding a storm in her hands, and she needs her anchor. Go, Roffel Tindle. Protect her while I move the world."

Chapter 15: Truths and Deceptions

Roffel sprinted back into the damp chill of the cave, his boots skidding on the mossy rocks. He was breathless, his chest swelling with the triumph of a son who had finally served his father.

Inside the blue-lit cavern, **Professor Sproun** sat motionless within Saerene's energy cage. Her silver-rimmed spectacles reflected the sapphire glow, making her eyes look like twin moons. Saerene stood guard, her face etched with exhaustion.

Roffel squared his shoulders, looking down at the prisoner. "It's over, Sproun," he said, his voice ringing with newfound authority. "I've delivered the map to my father. He is the Guardian of the Source. Even as we speak, he is rewriting the magic of the forest. You and your Dark Ones will never find the Hut now."

Sproun slowly tilted her head. A faint, jagged smile pulled at the corner of her mouth—not a smile of defeat, but one of pity. Then, she began to laugh. It was a dry, hollow sound that echoed off the stone walls like the rattling of old bones.

"Foolish, beautiful boy," she whispered, shaking her head. "You haven't saved the world. You've just handed the keys of the kingdom to the wolf."

The Hero's Mask Crumbles

Roffel flinched as if she had struck him. "I stopped you from using that map for your 'Veil' and your darkness," he snapped, his anger flaring.

Sproun's eyes flashed with a sudden, sharp intensity. "You think *I* am the villain? I spent sixteen years in the shadows. I changed my name, buried my past, and took a teaching job just to keep an eye on Warrick. I watched him every single day, waiting for his true face to slip."

She leaned against the bars of the blue cage, her gaze locking onto Roffel's. "And now you stand here, glowing with pride, telling me that the Butcher of Glowsky—the man known as **Tindle**—is your father?"

The air in the cave suddenly felt like ice. Roffel's stomach twisted into a cold knot. "You're lying. He saved me. He protected the school when the Vein was cut."

Sproun let out a long, weary sigh. "I sent that dog after you, Roffel. Not to kill you, but to draw blood. I needed to see if the map would react to you. I was trying to stall for time because I knew what would happen if that parchment ever reached his house."

Saerene stepped forward, her brow furrowed. "If you're a protector, why steal the map? Why hide?"

"Because I was trying to save a soul trapped in that Hut," Sproun said, her voice cracking with a hidden grief. "When Tindle found the location, he didn't guard it—he imprisoned it. He wove a shield around that Hut so thick that no one could enter or leave. I've been missing from school because I was out there, breaking my hands against his magic, trying to get in. He fed you stories, Roffel. He made you believe he was the hero of a war he actually started."

The North Star: Vein

Roffel's hands began to tremble. "He said the map was cursed... he said he couldn't touch it himself."

Sproun's eyes narrowed. "Of course he didn't touch it. The map was wove by the *real* Guardian to burn any hand filled with malice. He needed a true heir's blood to carry it across his threshold. The moment that map entered his house, it didn't just show the Hut. It revealed the one thing Tindle has craved for a thousand years."

She studied Roffel's pale face. "Tell me. When the sun hit that map in his study... what did you see in the North?"

Roffel's voice was barely a ghost. **"Vein."**

The word caused Saerene to gasp, her blue shield flickering for a second. Sproun's face turned deathly grim.

"Vein isn't a place, Roffel," Sproun whispered. "It is the Primordial Heart. The Hut is the old home of our ancestry where she was trapped and the Vein is the source of magic. It is the ocean. If Tindle reaches the North, he won't just be a Guardian. He will be a god. And a god with his heart has no room for a son."

The silence in the cave was absolute, broken only by the drip of water from the ceiling. Saerene looked from the caged professor to Roffel, then back again. A memory from the secret storeroom flashed in her mind—the dusty portrait of a woman with a gentle deer.

"You're **Grenstein**, aren't you?" Saerene asked, her voice filled with a sudden, crystalline certainty.

Sproun stiffened. The name seemed to physically pull the shadows away from her. "How... how do you know that name?"

"The portrait in the hidden chamber," Saerene said, stepping closer to the cage. "A woman holding a baby deer. A Protector of Knowledge. The one who was said to have vanished during the Great Betrayal." She looked into Sproun's weary, brilliant eyes. "It's you. You're the one Tindle couldn't kill."

Grenstein—the woman once known as Sproun—closed her eyes for a moment, a single tear tracing a path through the dust on her cheek. When she opened them, the "Professor" was gone. In her place stood an Ancient of Glowsky.

"I am Grenstein," she admitted softly. "And if you can find the courage to believe a 'villain,' I can show you how to stop Tindle before he drinks from the Vein and turns this world into a wasteland."

Roffel looked at his hands—the hands that had carried the map to the enemy. He felt the weight of his blood, a legacy he no longer understood. But as he looked at Saerene and the woman in the cage, he realized the truth was no longer in the books or the dreams. It was in the fight ahead.

"The cage," Roffel said, looking at Saerene. "Open it. We have a god to hunt."

Chapter 16: The Battle for Vein

The forest was a graveyard of silence as Roffel, Saerene, and the woman once known as Sproun—now revealed as the legendary **Grenstien**—stood before the mystic hut. It was no longer just a shack; it pulsed with a rhythmic, golden light, protected by a shimmering dome of energy that hummed like a thousand bees.

Grenstien stepped forward, her dark cloak swirling. She pressed her palms against the barrier, whispering incantations that had been forgotten for a century. The shield flared, rejecting her. Saerene tried next, her blue light lashing against the dome like waves against a cliff. Nothing.

Grenstien's shoulders slumped. For the first time, the fierce professor looked broken. "Warrick's—Tindle's—malice is too thick. He has woven his hate into the very molecules of this air. We are too late."

The Power of Three

Roffel stepped into the center. He didn't feel like a student anymore; he felt like a conductor at the center of a storm. "It's not over," he said, his voice dropping into a deep, commanding register.

He took Grenstien's hand on his left and Saerene's on his right. The moment their skin touched, a circuit closed. It wasn't just magic; it was a bridge of history, loyalty, and blood. A blinding white light exploded from their joined hands, a pillar of purity that slammed into the barrier.

With a sound like shattering diamonds, the shield disintegrated. The hut stood before them, its door creaking open as if letting out a long-held breath.

The Guardian in the Shadows

They descended the old ladder into the underground chamber, where the air was thick enough to taste. Symbols glowed along the walls, whispering secrets in a language only Roffel's blood could understand.

At the center of the room, bound by chains of invisible gravity, stood a woman. A glowing tiara rested on her brow, pulsing in sync with the heartbeat of the world. Her eyes, the exact shade of Roffel's, widened.

"You came," she whispered, her voice like silk and steel.

With a swift motion, Grenstien shattered the restraints. The woman stumbled forward, and as she looked at Roffel, the "Guardian" disappeared, leaving only her mother.

"That's not possible," she breathed, touching Roffel's face with trembling fingers. "You cracked the Lumivara? Only my blood... only my son..." Her voice broke into a choked sob as she pulled him into a fierce embrace. "Are you... my Roff?"

Roffel's world, which had been a spinning top of lies, finally stopped. The warmth of her hug was the only truth he needed. "You're my mother," he realized, the word feeling new and ancient at the same time.

"Tindle stole you from the cradle," Alaska cried into his shoulder. "He used your birthright to lock me away. But the magic remembered you, Roff. It waited for you to come home."

Flight of the Golden Dawn

"There is no time for tears," Alaska said, her face hardening into a mask of war. "Grenstien, I know the North. He is moving toward the Vein. If he drinks from the source, the world turns to ash."

Saerene looked at her in awe. "We saw your portrait, the one with the phoenix!"

Alaska smiled, a flash of her old power returning. She raised a hand toward the skylight, and a piercing, melodic cry tore through the night. A Phoenix—a creature of living gold and sun-fire—soared down from the clouds.

"We ride," Alaska commanded.

They climbed onto the creature's back, its feathers warm and vibrating with energy. As they soared over the forest, the world below changed. The green trees withered into a deep, unnatural violet as they approached the North.

"The school became ordinary because I was gone," Alaska shouted over the wind. "Without the Guardian, the magic has no anchor. We are the last line of defense."

The Battle Begins

The **Vein of Glowsky** pulsed beneath their feet, a valley of white crystalline stone that vibrated with the heavy, rhythmic heartbeat of the world. At its center, suspended in a pillar of shimmering light, sat the **Crystal of the Source**. It was a jagged, flawless diamond that hummed with a sound like a thousand choirs. This was the origin of all magic—the battery that powered every wand and every whispered spell in the world.

Roffel, Saerene, Grenstien and Alaska stood at the sacred ground's edge. The night air was thick with tension.

Roffel turned to Alaska. "We made it. What now?"

Alaska didn't hesitate. She lifted her hands.

A golden shockwave of energy burst into the sky, spiralling like a beacon.

A moment later—

Portals split open. Figures stepped forth.

Magicians, dressed in robes of emerald, crimson, indigo, and gold, emerged wands glowing, staffs crackling, relics pulsing with power.

The Professors of Glowsky.

Principal Harold Wood. His gaze was steely, determined.

 And many others—teachers, elders, warriors of magic—all answering Alaska's call.

Roffel's chest tightened. They weren't alone.

Saerene whispered, "This is it."

Then—the air turned cold.

A shadow slithered across the ground. A sudden gust of wind snuffed out some of the floating lanterns.

And then—laughter.

A deep, cruel chuckle echoed through the battlefield.

Tindle had arrived.

He strode forward, his blood-red cloak billowing behind him.

Behind him, dark magicians emerged like a tide—hooded figures with glowing red eyes, whispering dark incantations.

Tindle stopped a few feet away. His piercing gaze locked onto Roffel.

Then, a slow, mocking smirk spread across his face.

"Oh… you got here before me but now there is no need to hide the vein again," he said, his voice smooth yet venomous. His eyes flickered with amusement. "Tell me, Alaska… how does it feel to stand before me? After all, … I was the one who captured you—sixteen years ago."

Roffel froze.

A flood of emotions hit him all at once.

Saerene's grip tightened around his hand. She stepped forward, her voice firm. "You talk too much."

Tindle chuckled. "And you always rush into battle. That's what makes this so fun."

Then—his gaze flicked to Alaska.

"You, dear guardian… you truly think you've won? Even with all your little friends?" His voice turned sharp. "You are weak now"

Alaska's expression didn't waver.

"You hold power, Tindle," she said calmly. "But you are not magic."

Tindle's smirk faltered, just for a second. Roffel turned to his mother. His voice was desperate.

"Mother, you're the Guardian of Glowsky. Use the Crystal of Veil! You have the right—you can defeat him!"

Alaska turned to her son, her face sorrowful but firm.

"No, Roffel."

Roffel blinked. "Why? You're the Guardian! You protect magic, don't you?"

Alaska placed a gentle hand on his shoulder.

"I can't use the crystal directly, Roffel," she said softly. "There is only one way for me to use its power—I would have to soak it into myself."

Roffel's heart pounded. "Then do it! It's the only way to stop him!"

Alaska shook her head. "I am a Guardian. My duty is to protect the crystal, not distort or destroy it. If I soak its power, I become like Tindle. I take what is meant to remain pure." Then—Alaska lifted her hand.

Chapter 17: The Rise of Glowsky

The air over the Vein didn't just stand still; it felt heavy, like a physical weight pressing against the lungs of every warrior present. It was the suffocating quiet that precedes a hurricane—a moment where the world holds its breath before the first drop of blood hits the white stone.

The scent of ozone and ancient, disturbed earth hung thick in the air. Overhead, the sky was a bruised purple, clouds coiling like serpents charged with the static of ten thousand spells.

Roffel stood at the epicenter of the tension, his heart hammering a frantic rhythm against his ribs. He watched his mother, Alaska, standing like a pillar of living gold, her aura a beacon that refused to flicker. He watched Saerene, her hands glowing with sapphire light, and Grenstien, her face a mask of iron resolve.

Frustration, hot and bitter, rose in his throat. *I am the son of a Queen and a Tyrant,* he thought, *and yet I am a spectator.*

The Mirror of the Soul

"I have nothing," Roffel whispered, his voice cracking. "No spells. No staves. No incantations. How am I supposed to stand in this storm?"

Saerene turned to him. In the midst of the chaos, her violet eyes were unnervingly calm. She didn't look at him with pity; she looked at him with recognition.

"Why do you insist on being blind, Roffel?" she asked, her voice a steady anchor.

Roffel exhaled a jagged breath. "Because I can't *do* anything! I don't have charms, I don't have a wand—"

"Magic isn't a tool you pick up, Roffel," Saerene interrupted, stepping closer until the heat of her own power warmed his skin. "It's the blood in your veins. It's the way your skin knit itself back together in that cave without a single word being spoken. It's the way the shield of the Hut didn't just break—it *recognized* you and stepped aside."

Grenstien stepped forward, her sharp features softening. "She is right, Roffel. I spent years watching you, waiting for a spark, thinking you were just a boy caught in a man's war. But the spark was always there. You didn't lack magic; you were just afraid to let it burn."

The Tyrant's Scorn

A slow, rhythmic clapping echoed across the white stones of the Vein, cutting through the wind like a knife.

"A touching sentiment," Tindle sneered, stepping out from the swirling black mist. His blood-red cloak billowed behind him, looking like a fresh wound against the white valley. "But foolish. You think blood alone makes a King? Magic isn't a birthright, boy. It is a prize for the one strong enough to seize it."

Tindle's eyes locked onto Roffel's, his smirk widening into something jagged and cruel. "You are a vessel with no wine. A crown with no head. Watch how a *real* master commands the Source."

With a violent roar, Tindle slammed his staff into the ground. A wave of absolute darkness exploded outward, turning the silver moonlight into a void.

The War of the Ages

The Vein shuddered. The ancient rift of magic beneath their feet pulsed with a raw, untamed energy that made the very air scream. This was no longer a skirmish in the woods; it was a war for the architecture of reality.

Alaska stepped forward, her golden light expanding until it pushed back the shadows. "You will never lay a hand on the Crystal of the Vein, Tindle. Not while I draw breath."

Tindle chuckled, a sound of pure, unadulterated malice. "Oh, my dear Guardian... you of all people should know that destiny is written in lead, not gold. Crystal has been waiting for me for sixteen years. It is tired of your 'protection.' It wants to be used."

Alaska's expression turned to stone, her eyes blazing with the light of a thousand suns. "Then come and take it. If you can survive the dawn."

And with that, the sky didn't just break—it shattered.

Alaska unleashed a golden shockwave that met Tindle's darkness in a deafening crack of thunder. From the portals behind them, the Professors of Glowsky charged, their wands casting streaks of emerald and indigo across the gloom. From the black mist, the hooded acolytes of Tindle lunged forward, their red eyes glowing like hot coals.

Roffel felt the vibration of the Crystal deep in his marrow. He looked at his hands, and for the first time, he didn't see a boy. He saw a conduit. The war for the future had begun, and the Heir of Glowsky was finally ready to stop watching and start leading.

The battle began.

The battlefield was a storm of noise and light. Red, blue, and gold spells shot through the air like fireworks, cutting through the dark sky. Every time the magic crashed together, the ground shook, and the heavy stones under their feet began to crack.

The magicians of Glowsky fought with everything they had. Principal and Grenstein stood firm, creating glowing shields to protect their friends from the dark attacks. Saerene's blue magic moved through the air like glowing silk, stopping the curses sent by Tindle's followers.

Alaska was at the front, leading the charge. Her golden magic was bright and fast, hitting the dark magicians with perfect aim. But Tindle's army would not stop. Shadows moved across the ground like living snakes, twisting around the warriors. The fight was a tie—until Roffel saw something strange.

In the middle of the chaos, a shadow was moving toward the Vein's sacred chamber. It wasn't a monster. It was one of their own people.

The Betrayal

Inside the chamber, the air was thick with power. At the center of the room, the Crystal of Vein floated in the air, glowing with ancient light.

The figure stopped for a second, hesitating. Then, with a quick move, they grabbed the crystal and ran back toward the battlefield. No one saw it happen at first.

Then, a loud, cruel laugh echoed across the field. Roffel's heart skipped a beat. Tindle held out his hand, and the hooded figure placed the glowing Crystal into his palm.

A heavy silence fell over the battlefield. The warriors of Glowsky stopped fighting, frozen in shock. Horror spread through them like a cold fog. Someone had betrayed them.

Alaska didn't wait. She fired a bolt of golden energy at the traitor's feet. The blast blew away the dust and forced the figure to show his face.

The hood fell back. It was Varkis.

Everyone gasped. Alaska's eyes went wide, and her voice was a trembling whisper. *"Varkis... we trusted you."*

The man who had fought beside them—the father of Tissa Varkis—stood there as a traitor once again. Tindle gripped the crystal tightly, a dark smile on his face.

"Well done, old friend," Tindle said.

The Silent Void

The moment Tindle's fingers closed around the **Crystal of Vein**, the world seemed to scream. A shockwave of oily, black energy exploded outward, washing over the battlefield like a cold tide.

Then came the silence.

One by one, the lights of Glowsky went out. The Principal's massive shield didn't just break—it evaporated into thin mist. Grenstein's ancient staff, which had glowed for decades, turned into a dull piece of wood. Saerene stumbled, her hands trembling as she felt the warmth leave her veins. Her magic was gone.

The warriors of Glowsky stood like statues, hollow and powerless.

Tindle let out a jagged, dark laugh. He flexed his fingers, and the stolen power danced around him like black flames. "I have waited a lifetime for this," he hissed. "Look at you. Without your magic, you are just fragile humans. Now, watch as I erase what is left of you."

Hope didn't just fade; it shattered like glass. Tindle raised his hand, his eyes glowing with a cruel light, ready to end the war with a single strike.

The Heart's Spark

But then, a sound broke the hopelessness. **The sound of footsteps.**

Roffel stepped forward. He wasn't glowing. He didn't have a weapon. But his eyes were steady.

"Is this all we are?" Roffel's voice rang out, clear and sharp against the wind. He looked at his fallen friends. "Do we truly disappear just because our hands are empty?"

The battlefield went deathly quiet.

"Magic was never just a tool we picked up," Roffel continued, his voice growing stronger. "It wasn't just in our wands or our spells. It was in our choice to protect each other. It was in our will to stand up when the world told us to stay down!"

Tindle sneered, his face twisting in anger. "And what will a powerless boy do?"

He flicked his wrist, hurling a bolt of pure, crushing darkness straight at Roffel's chest. It moved like a predator. But the moment it touched him—

CLANG.

A shield of brilliant gold erupted from nowhere. It wasn't coming from a wand; it was pouring out of Roffel's very soul. Tindle's eyes widened in horror. He attacked again, faster and harder.

Flash. Flash. Flash.

Every dark spell hit a wall of golden light.

The Roar of Glowsky

Around the field, the air began to hum. It started as a tiny spark in the palm of a young student, then a flicker in Grenstein's eyes. The staff in his hand began to pulse with a heartbeat of light.

Tindle staggered back, the Crystal vibrating violently in his grip. "No… this is impossible! I drained the Vein! I took it all!"

Grenstein stepped forward, a smirk touching her lips. "You stole the water, Tindle," she said softly, "but you forgot that we are the spring."

Saerene's bluish light returned, swirling around her like a protective storm. "Magic isn't just a battery you can drain," she said, her voice echoing with power. "It is a belief. It is the love we have for this world. And we still believe."

The battlefield didn't just glow—it **roared**. The darkness was pushed back by a thousand individual suns as the magicians of Glowsky realized that their greatest power wasn't a gift from the Crystal.

It was a gift they gave to themselves.

The Final Strike

Tindle, consumed by rage, gathered every ounce of his remaining strength. With a roar, he hurled one last, desperate bolt of dark energy at the group.

Saerene reacted instantly, throwing a powerful counter-spell—but in the chaos, her aim flickered. The bolt of light streaked past Tindle's shoulder, hitting nothing but air.

Tindle let out a jagged, cruel laugh. "Oh, little girl... your aim is as pathetic as your—"

He froze. The laugh died in his throat.

Alaska hadn't just watched. She had moved like a flash of gold. She didn't block the dark magic; she reached out and caught the raw energy with her bare hands. With a graceful, powerful spin, she redirected the bolt. It didn't hit the ground—it tore straight back into Tindle.

Tindle screamed as his own malice burned him.

Beside her, Roffel reached out and clasped his mother's hand. Together, their combined spirits created a golden wave that erupted across the field. Tindle fell to his knees, his strength shattered.

With a dull thud, the Crystal of Vein slipped from Tindle's trembling fingers, hitting the dark soil.

Weak and broken, Tindle looked up at them. A twisted, terrifying grin spread across his pale lips. His voice was a dying whisper:

"I will be back."

And with a sudden flicker of shadow, he vanished into the air.

The Restoration

The silence that followed was heavy. Alaska exhaled, her shoulders dropping from exhaustion, but her face was serene. She walked toward the Vein, where the whole, glowing Crystal still pulsed faintly in the earth.

Standing like a true Guardian, she raised her hands and whispered the ancient words of restoration. The Crystal lifted into the air, its light growing so bright it blinded everyone. The earth hummed, and the very essence of magic poured back into the roots of the school.

The shadows melted away. The sky cleared from a bruised purple to a soft, warm orange. The balance was finally restored.

Glowsky rose again.

Roffel took a deep breath, feeling the magic of the school welcoming him home. He wasn't just an outsider anymore. He was Roffel Grayson, and his journey was only just beginning.

The Bittersweet Sunset

The sun was setting, painting the grand school of magic in shades of gold. The towering spires of Glowsky shimmered, and the stone walls seemed to breathe with life after years of slumber.

Everywhere, there was movement. Students in colorful robes filled the pathways, their laughter echoing against the great archways. You could feel the excitement in the air—the school was alive.

Roffel stood with his friends—Saerene, Kael, and Marush. They watched the beautiful scene, but they didn't join in the cheering. A heavy, painful silence sat between them.

They had won the battle. They had saved the school. But as they looked at the sunset, they all felt the same empty space in their circle.

Lila.

The Search for Lila

Kael finally broke the heavy silence. His voice was sharp with worry. "What about Lila? We've searched every corner of the school. She wouldn't just vanish into thin air."

Roffel didn't look away from the horizon. He had been replaying every memory of the past few days, and finally, the pieces clicked into place. His gaze was steady, his voice low. "I know exactly where she is."

Marush frowned, crossing his arms. "And how exactly do you know that?"

Roffel didn't explain. Instead, a small, knowing smirk touched his lips. "Just trust me."

Saerene, Kael, and Marush exchanged nervous glances. They had followed Roffel through fire and shadows before; they weren't going to stop now.

The Cursed Estate

Together, they left the safety of Glowsky's glowing walls and headed toward a place that felt like a scar on the land: The abandoned estate of Warrick Tindle.

The stone mansion loomed ahead like a giant skeleton. Once grand and imposing, it was now a crumbling relic. Thick vines crawled up the walls like reaching fingers, and the silence around the house felt heavy and unnatural—as if the birds were too afraid to sing there.

The massive wooden doors groaned in protest as Roffel pushed them open. Inside, the air tasted of dust and old secrets. Cobwebs draped over forgotten statues like ghostly veils. The shelves were cluttered with strange magical trinkets and the dusty remains of dark spells.

Marush shivered, his eyes darting to the shadows. "This place gives me the creeps. It feels like the house is watching us."

The Unlocking

In the center of the main hall, Saerene moved toward a heavy wooden box sitting on a large, scarred table. It was wrapped in ancient runes that pulsed with a faint, sickly light.

"This is it," she whispered, her voice echoing in the empty room.

Kael stepped forward, rolling up his sleeves. "Then let's break this thing open."

Saerene raised her hands, her fingers weaving a complex unlocking spell. The runes flickered, fighting back for a moment, before they finally shattered like thin glass.

The lid flew off, and a swirl of pale blue mist poured out, smelling of cold winter air. A figure tumbled forward from the mist. Roffel moved like lightning, catching her before she hit the floor.

Lila.

Her eyes were wide with shock, her chest heaving as she breathed in the dusty air. "I... I was trapped there for days! It was so dark..."

Saerene placed a warm, reassuring hand on her shoulder. "Breathe, Lila. You're safe now."

Lila's voice trembled as she looked at Roffel. "Warrick... he put me in there. He kept asking about the hidden passages of Glowsky. He was looking for something... and I found what it was."

Roffel's jaw tightened. He looked around the decaying room, his eyes cold. "It doesn't matter anymore," he said firmly. "He's gone. His secrets stay in the dust."

Lila took a shaky breath and nodded, leaning on her friends for support. With their circle finally complete again, they turned their backs on the darkness of the past and walked toward the light of their true home—**Glowsky**.

The Gift of the Vein

The halls of Glowsky were no longer cold and silent. They were vibrating with life. Everywhere you looked, the air was filled with golden laughter, the hum of spells, and the excited whispers of a thousand secrets. In the sun-drenched courtyard, students were practicing their crafts; some woven shimmering shields that looked like soap bubbles, while others summoned tiny, swirling tornados or bursts of bright fire that danced on their fingertips.

Marush and Kael stood by the ancient stone fountain, their eyes wide as they watched a first-year student make a heavy book float in mid-air.

Marush let out a long, heavy breath. "We should have been here since the beginning," he said, his voice trailing off.

Roffel turned to him, curious. "What do you mean?"

Kael looked down at his own empty hands, hesitating before he spoke. "We come from magical families, Roffel. Our blood carries the old stories. But when the Vein was cut off, the magic in our homes just... died. Our parents lost their sparks. Their staves became ordinary wood. Because of that, they never had anything to pass down to us."

Saerene frowned, her heart aching for them. "So, you grew up surrounded by the *idea* of magic, but you never learned a single spell?"

Kael shook his head slowly. "Not one. Not even a light to guide us in the dark."

Marush crossed his arms, but a new light was flickering in his eyes as he watched the fountain's water dance to a student's command. "But now that the Vein is pulsing again... now that Glowsky is breathing... we finally have a chance to claim what was stolen from us."

Roffel felt the weight of their words. He reached out, placing a firm, reassuring hand on each of their shoulders. He looked at the grand spires of the school and then back at his brothers-in-arms.

"Then we don't look back," Roffel said with a steady smile. "From today, we will learn together. We build our own legends."

The Two Mothers

That evening, the Grand Hall of Glowsky was quiet, filled only with the soft amber glow of fading sunlight. Roffel walked across the polished stone floor, his footsteps echoing. At the far end of the hall, **Alaska Greyson** stood waiting, her golden robes shimmering like a quiet flame.

Beside her, another woman stepped out from the shadows. She wore plain, simple clothes that looked out of place in a magical palace, and she carried no wand or staff. Yet, she stood with a quiet strength that filled the room.

Ellen.

She was the woman who had tucked Roffel into bed every night, the one who had healed his scraped knees and taught him how to be kind.

Ellen hesitated, her eyes misting over as she looked at Alaska. She began to bow, her voice trembling. "I was only a servant in your house... yet you trusted me with the most precious thing you owned. You gave me your son."

Alaska's fierce expression melted away, replaced by a look of deep, ancient gratitude. "I didn't just give him to a servant, Ellen. I gave him to a soul I knew would love him more than the world itself. Thank you for raising my son."

Ellen sank to her knees, her voice thick with tears. "I only did what was right. I promised to keep the spark alive."

Roffel felt his heart hammer against his ribs like a trapped bird. The truth was finally out in the open. "You... you were my mother's servant?" he asked, his voice barely a whisper.

Ellen nodded slowly. "Alaska knew the shadows were coming, Roffel. She knew the war would take everything. She chose to lose you so that you could grow up safe, far away from the spells and the blood."

Roffel looked from the legendary Queen of Magic to the humble woman who had raised him in the dirt and the sun. He didn't hesitate. He stepped forward and gently took Ellen's rough, hardworking hands in his own.

"The blood in my veins might belong to a legend," Roffel said, his voice steady and warm, "but my heart belongs to you. You are my mother, Ellen. No crown or spell will ever change that."

A tear rolled down Alaska's cheek as she smiled—not as a Queen, but as a mother who had finally seen her son come home.

The Weight of Gold and Shadow

The morning sun hit the spires of Glowsky, turning the entire school into a beacon of light. Inside, the halls were a river of moving robes and excited chatter. The air smelled of old parchment and the faint, sweet scent of ozone—the smell of magic returning to the world.

But as Roffel and his friends moved toward the Great Hall, the air turned cold. Three students blocked their path, their expensive robes perfectly pressed and their faces twisted into arrogant smirks.

Jace Korran, **Tessa Varkis**, and **Gav Renn**.

Jace stepped forward, his eyes locking onto Roffel with a look of pure disdain. "Well, well," Jace sneered, his voice loud enough for other students to hear. "If it isn't the 'Little Guardian' himself. Tell us, Roffel, does the crown feel heavy on such a common head?"

Tessa, the daughter of the traitor Varkis, let out a sharp, mocking laugh. "I'm surprised you survived the night, Roffel. I thought the darkness would have swallowed someone as... ordinary as you."

Marush's face turned red, and his fists clenched at his sides. "Shut it, Tessa. Leave him alone before you regret it."

Jace's grin widened, becoming something sharper and more dangerous. "Oh? You think you're so brave? Tell me, Roffel... have you ever wondered how **Miss Harrow** found you that night in the woods? Do you really think it was an accident?" His eyes gleamed with a secret. "Think about who pointed her in your direction."

Roffel's breath caught in his throat. His eyes narrowed as a thousand questions flooded his mind. What was Jace implying? Before he could step forward to demand an answer, a voice like rolling thunder shook the hallway.

"Enough."

The crowd of students parted instantly. **Principal Harold Wood** stood at the top of the marble stairs. He didn't need a wand to look powerful; his very presence was like a wall of iron.

"Today is not a day for petty grudges or division," Harold said, his voice firm and commanding. "It is a day for a new beginning. The Vein is open, and the law of this school is simple: Knowledge is earned, not inherited."

He gestured toward the long table at the front of the hall. "I present to you the masters of your craft."

One by one, the legendary figures stepped forward. **Grenstein** leaned on his staff, which now glowed with a steady, ancient light. Behind him stood the other masters of the elements. The students erupted into a roar of cheers that shook the windows.

Magic had truly returned to Glowsky, but so had the secrets. As the golden light filled the hall, Roffel realized that while the war with Tindle was over, the battle for the truth was just beginning.

Final Chapter: The Missing Piece

Shadows of the Founders

The war was over, and the scars on the earth had begun to heal. **Glowsky** had returned to its former glory—a golden fortress where magic flowed as freely as water in a river. The classrooms were loud with the voices of eager students, and a fragile peace had settled over the land like a warm blanket.

But for **Roffel**, the silence was louder than the cheering. Even with the sun shining, a cold shadow lingered in the back of his mind. Something was still missing.

Late that night, he sat in the **Guardian's Chamber**. Across from him sat his mother, **Alaska Greyson**, her golden robes reflecting the orange glow of the crackling fireplace. The fire hissed and popped, casting long, dancing shadows against the ancient stone walls.

Roffel's fingers drummed restlessly against the heavy wooden table. He looked at the flickering flames, then finally met his mother's gaze.

"Mother… there are things that don't make sense. I need to know the truth."

Alaska leaned forward, her eyes soft but curious. "The war is won, Roffel. What still troubles your heart?"

He hesitated, the memory of his visions flashing behind his eyes. "In my dreams—the ones that guided me here—I saw a woman. Her name was **Mathelda**. She was always there, watching from the corners of the room. But when I finally found the hut from my vision... she was gone. Everything else was exactly the same, but she had vanished."

At the mention of that name, the air in the room seemed to turn ice-cold. Alaska stiffened, her regal posture becoming even sharper. Her eyes widened with a shock she couldn't hide.

"**Mathelda?**" she whispered, the name sounding like a prayer and a warning all at once.

Roffel nodded urgently. "You know her. Who was she?"

Alaska took a long, slow breath, as if gathering the weight of centuries. "Mathelda was not just a sorceress, Roffel. She was one of the **Original Three**—the founders who first bled their magic into the earth to create the Vein and the Crystal. She is the very reason Glowsky exists."

Roffel frowned, his mind spinning. "But if she is a founder, she should be a legend in a book. Why was she in my head? Why was she showing me the way?"

Alaska's face clouded with a deep, dark worry. "That is what frightens me, my son. Mathelda has been gone from this world for hundreds of years. If her spirit has stepped out of the mist to speak to you... it means the battle with Tindle was only the beginning. It means a much older door has been opened."

A heavy, suffocating silence filled the chamber. The fire in the hearth flickered lower, turning from bright orange to a dying, ghostly blue.

The Master's Blueprint

Suddenly, a realization struck Roffel like a bolt of lightning. He leaned over the table, his eyes wide.

"The map," he whispered. "Mother, I've been thinking about the parchment that led us through the forest. What was its *true* purpose? It felt like it was alive."

Alaska's face grew grave, the firelight catching the sharp lines of her royal features.

"The map was never meant to be a guide to a hiding place," she admitted, her voice low. "In the beginning, it was the Original Blueprint of the Vein. Roffel felt his stomach tighten into a knot. "Then how did it lead us straight to your hut? If it was a map of the whole world, why did it point to one tiny door?"

A sad, knowing smile touched Alaska's lips. It was the smile of a Queen who had outsmarted a King.

"Because I **rewrote** it," she said simply.

Roffel blinked, leaning back in shock. "You... you changed a Founder's map?"

Alaska nodded slowly. "I used my own life-force to bend the ink and alter its course. I turned a global map into a private compass. I knew that one day, my sister or a true ally would come looking for me. Tindle was obsessed with that map—he thought he held the key to the world's power—but he never understood its true nature."

Roffel took a step closer, his voice urgent. "And when Tindle stole it? What happened then?"

Alaska's gaze darkened, and for a moment, the fire in the hearth turned a deep, vengeful purple.

"I didn't just change it, Roffel. **I cursed it.**"

A cold shiver ran down Roffel's spine. "You turned it against him?"

"Exactly," she replied. "The moment Tindle's dark magic touched that parchment, it became a labyrinth with no exit. The map didn't guide him anymore; it lied to him. It whispered false directions and led him in circles, keeping him lost in his own greed while we prepared for the final strike. He thought he was the hunter, but the map made him the prey."

Roffel exhaled a long breath he didn't know he was holding. It all made sense now. Tindle hadn't been defeated just by spells on a battlefield—he had been defeated by a mother's shadow-play months before the first spark was even thrown.

The Secret in the Glass

The battlefield was finally still, though the air still tasted of ozone and ancient power. Tindle was gone, his shadow pulled back into the void, but his final threat—*I will be back*—seemed to hang in the mist like a cold promise.

Roffel leaned against a ruined stone, his muscles aching with an exhaustion that went deeper than bone. He watched his mother, Alaska Greyson, as she stood over the pulsing heart of the Vein.

"You asked me once," Alaska said, her voice calm and steady, "why didn't I use the Crystal to end this sooner."

Roffel looked up, his eyes narrowing. "You said you couldn't use it directly. That the power would distort you."

Alaska reached down and picked up the glowing stone. "The truth is simpler, Roffel. The Crystal was never whole."

Roffel took a step back, his mind racing to piece the puzzle together. "But... It looked perfect. It felt complete."

"A beautiful illusion," Alaska smiled. She turned to him, her golden eyes full of a new curiosity. "Which brings me to my own question. To find me, you had to break the seal on the Map. To do that, you needed the Lumvara—the concentrated light of a thousand suns. How did you manage that without the Crystal's core?"

Roffel blinked. He remembered that afternoon clearly. "Saerene used her glass necklace. She used it like a lens to catch the sun's rays and intensify them until the seal melted."

Alaska nodded slowly. "I used an old magic to create that seal. Nothing should have been strong enough to crack it except the core of the Vein itself."

The Law of Reflection

Roffel's heart began to pound. He felt like he was standing on the edge of a cliff, looking down at a truth that changed the entire world. But Alaska wasn't finished.

"Think back to the final strike," she said. "When Tindle absorbed the Crystal's energy, he thought he was a god. Saerene fired her most powerful spell—and it curved away. You thought she missed. Was it a bad aim, Roffel?"

Roffel's gaze darkened as the memory played back in slow motion. "No. It wasn't a mistake. The spell didn't miss... it was repelled. It was like a magnet pushing away its own kind."

"Exactly," Alaska explained, her voice dropping to a whisper. "Because the same power cannot destroy itself."

Roffel's mind reeled. He remembered how Grenstein's power had shattered the hut's shield, and how their magic returned even after Tindle drained the Vein. Everything clicked into place with a sudden, brilliant flash.

The Final Piece

His voice trembled as he looked at his mother. "What are you trying to say?"

Alaska gave a knowing, triumphant smile. "Tindle thought he had stolen the soul of Glowsky. But he only held half of the heart. The other half was never in the Vein. It was hidden in plain sight, carried by someone."

Roffel exhaled, the realization hitting him like a physical weight. "The missing fragment of the Crystal... it's in Saerene's necklace."

A stunned silence fell over the clearing. The "glass" necklace wasn't glass at all. It was the missing core—the reason their magic could never truly be stolen, and the reason Tindle could never truly win.

A wide, disbelieving grin spread across Roffel's face. "It looks like magic has always been one step ahead of us."

Alaska laughed softly, a sound of pure relief. "Magic isn't just power, Roffel—it's fate."

As the first true sun of peace began to rise over the spires of Glowsky, the battle was officially over. But as Roffel looked at his friends, he knew their story wasn't ending.

It was just the beginning.

***